Dear Parents and Educators,

Welcome to Penguin Young Readers! As parents and educators, you know that each child develops at his or her own pace—in terms of speech, critical thinking, and, of course, reading. Penguin Young Readers recognizes this fact. As a result, each Penguin Young Readers book is assigned a traditional easy-to-read level (1–4) as well as a Guided Reading Level (A–P). Both of these systems will help you choose the right book for your child. Please refer to the back of each book for specific leveling information. Penguin Young Readers features esteemed authors and illustrators, stories about favorite characters, fascinating nonfiction, and more!

Love Is in the Air

LEVEL **2**

GUIDED READING LEVEL **H**

This book is perfect for a **Progressing Reader** who:
- can figure out unknown words by using picture and context clues;
- can recognize beginning, middle, and ending sounds;
- can make and confirm predictions about what will happen in the text; and
- can distinguish between fiction and nonfiction.

Here are some **activities** you can do during and after reading this book:
- Picture Clues: Go through the book and match the pictures to the words. For example, point to the picture of Balloon and read the word *balloon* in the story.
- Retelling: What is the story about? What happens at the beginning, middle, and end of the story? Pay close attention to how Balloon is feeling. At first he is lonely, but how does his attitude shift throughout the story?

Remember, sharing the love of reading with a child is the best gift you can give!

—Bonnie Bader, EdM
  Penguin Young Readers program

*Penguin Young Readers are leveled by independent reviewers applying the standards developed by Irene Fountas and Gay Su Pinnell in *Matching Books to Readers: Using Leveled Books in Guided Reading*, Heinemann, 1999.

For Pendy, Coco, and Lulu,
who keep me aloft—JF

Penguin Young Readers
Published by the Penguin Group
Penguin Group (USA) Inc., 375 Hudson Street, New York, New York 10014, USA
Penguin Group (Canada), 90 Eglinton Avenue East, Suite 700, Toronto, Ontario M4P 2Y3, Canada
(a division of Pearson Penguin Canada Inc.)
Penguin Books Ltd., 80 Strand, London WC2R 0RL, England
Penguin Group Ireland, 25 St. Stephen's Green, Dublin 2, Ireland (a division of Penguin Books Ltd.)
Penguin Group (Australia), 250 Camberwell Road, Camberwell, Victoria 3124, Australia
(a division of Pearson Australia Group Pty. Ltd.)
Penguin Books India Pvt. Ltd., 11 Community Centre, Panchsheel Park, New Delhi—110 017, India
Penguin Group (NZ), 67 Apollo Drive, Rosedale, Auckland 0632, New Zealand
(a division of Pearson New Zealand Ltd.)
Penguin Books (South Africa) (Pty.) Ltd., 24 Sturdee Avenue, Rosebank,
Johannesburg 2196, South Africa
Penguin Books Ltd., Registered Offices: 80 Strand, London WC2R 0RL, England

Library of Congress Control Number: 2011046785

ISBN 978-0-448-49647-4 (pbk)   10 9 8 7 6 5 4 3 2 1
ISBN 978-0-448-46160-1 (hc)   10 9 8 7 6 5 4 3 2 1

LOVE IS IN THE AIR

by Jonathan Fenske

Penguin Young Readers
An Imprint of Penguin Group (USA) Inc.

The cake was gone.

The boys and girls were home.

But Balloon was still tied

to the table.

He was alone.

He started to droop.

5

Then came a gust of wind
and a new friend.

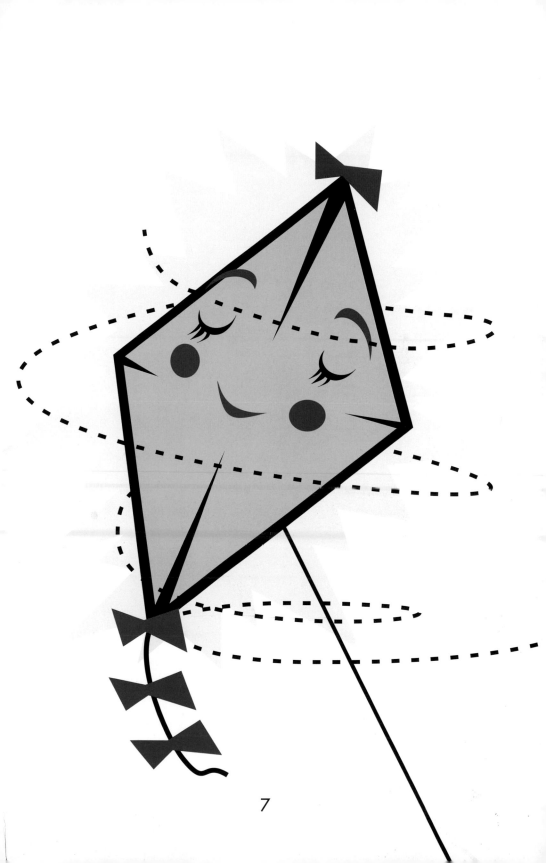

Come with me!

said Kite.

She rose on the breeze.

Wait for me! said Balloon.

He pulled.

And he pulled.

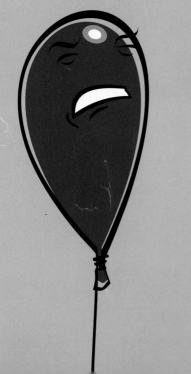

SNAP!

Until he was free.

Hello!

said Kite.

Hi!

said Balloon.

13

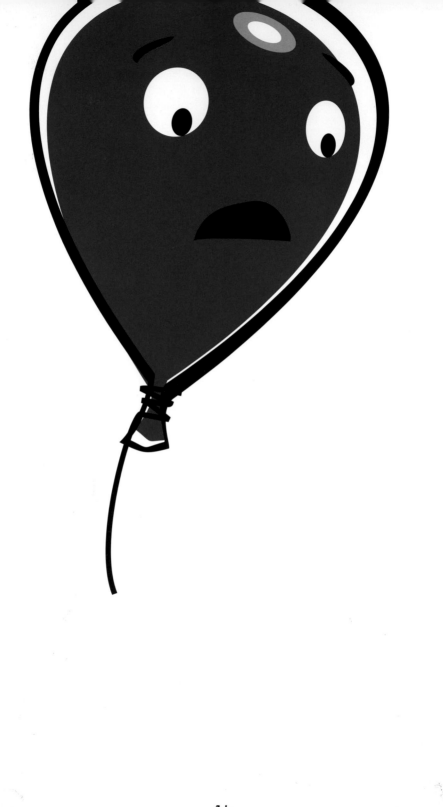

Balloon went up and up.

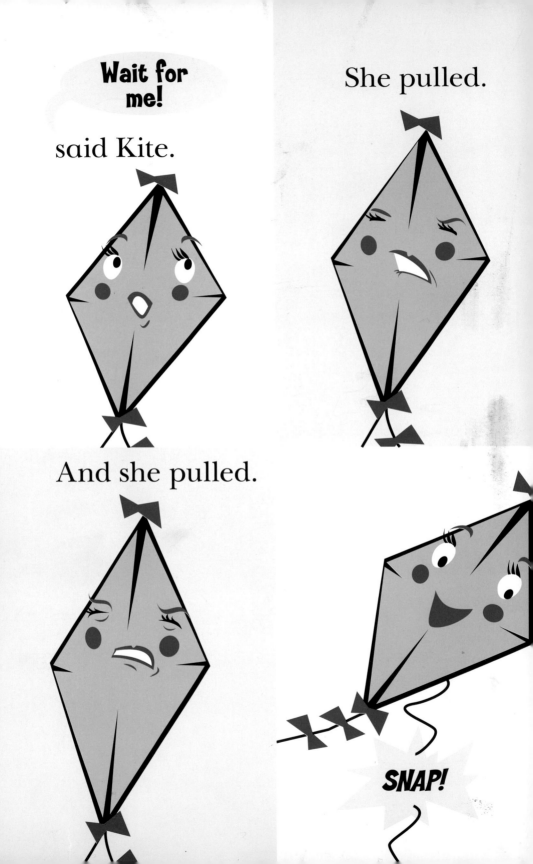

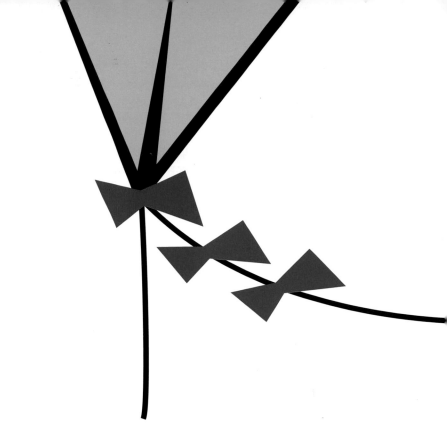

Until she was free.

At last they were side by side.

They flipped.

They dipped.

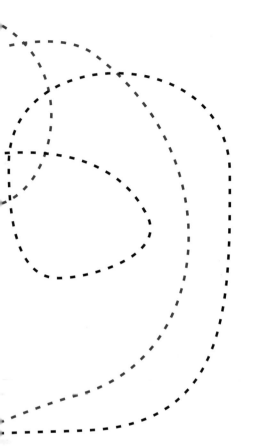

They spun in the wind.

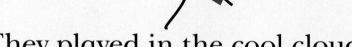

They played in the cool clouds.

They rested in the warm sun.

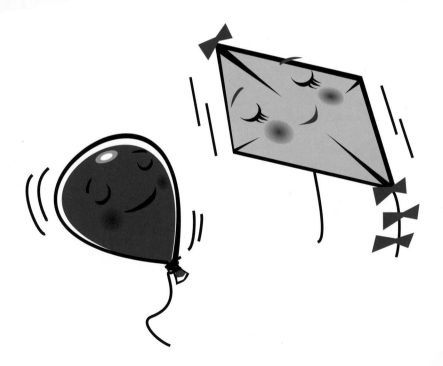

It was all such fun.

Uh-oh.

Until the wind stopped blowing.

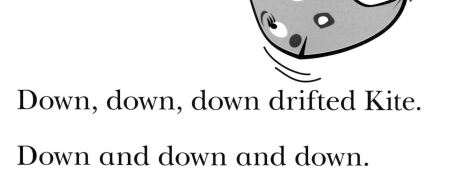

Down, down, down drifted Kite.

Down and down and down.

25

She landed in the branches

of a tall tree.

Balloon did not fall.

He kept going up.

Up and up and up.

He was so sad.

He missed his friend.

He did not see the bird.

And the bird did not see him.

Down, down, down went Balloon.

Down and down and down.

It was such a long way down.

He was dizzy.

He was scared.

At last he landed.

PLOP!

And Kite was there to catch him.